Hello!

This book belongs to

_____

I'm **walking**,
Going to Zanzibar!

And I'm **talking**
Like a movie star!

My Very First
100 Words

Selected, adapted, and illustrated by

ROSEMARY WELLS

A Paula Wiseman Book
Simon & Schuster Books for Young Readers
New York   London   Toronto   Sydney   New Delhi

honk

SIMON & SCHUSTER BOOKS FOR YOUNG READERS
An imprint of Simon & Schuster Children's Publishing Division
1230 Avenue of the Americas, New York, New York 10020
© 2022 by Rosemary Wells
Book design by Laurent Linn © 2022 by Simon & Schuster, Inc.
All rights reserved, including the right of reproduction in whole or in part in any form.
SIMON & SCHUSTER BOOKS FOR YOUNG READERS and related marks
are trademarks of Simon & Schuster, Inc.
For information about special discounts for bulk purchases, please contact Simon & Schuster Special Sales
at 1-866-506-1949 or business@simonandschuster.com.
The Simon & Schuster Speakers Bureau can bring authors to your live event.
For more information or to book an event, contact the Simon & Schuster Speakers Bureau at 1-866-248-3049
or visit our website at www.simonspeakers.com.
The text for this book was set in Banda Regular.
The illustrations for this book were rendered in watercolor paints, colored inks, self-made rubber stamps,
Copic markers, colored pencils, and watercolor pencils.
Manufactured in China
1221 SCP
First Edition
2 4 6 8 10 9 7 5 3 1
Library of Congress Cataloging-in-Publication Data
Names: Wells, Rosemary, author, illustrator.
Title: My very first 100 words / Rosemary Wells.
Other titles: My very first one hundred words | Mother Goose.
Description: First edition. | New York : Simon & Schuster Books for Young Readers, 2022. | "A Paula Wiseman book."
| Audience: Ages 0–8. | Audience: Grades K1. | Summary: Illustrated nursery rhymes highlight words for
parts of speech, actions, colors, numbers, opposites, greetings, and more. Includes a note from the author.
Identifiers: LCCN 2021008158 (print) | LCCN 2021008159 (ebook)
| ISBN 9781665901161 (hardcover) | ISBN 9781665901178 (ebook)
Subjects: LCSH: Nursery rhymes. | Children's poetry. | Vocabulary—Juvenile literature.
| CYAC: Nursery rhymes. | Vocabulary.
Classification: LCC PZ8.3.W465 My 2022 (print) | LCC PZ8.3.W465 (ebook) |DDC 398.8—dc23
LC record available at https://lccn.loc.gov/2021008158
LC ebook record available at https://lccn.loc.gov/2021008159

A Note from the Author

In this book I set out to support the way children really learn to speak, keeping in mind that children don't learn language one word at a time. Rhymes and their rhythm and repetition play an important role in developing verbal skills in children. The daily speech that every child encounters is a circus of activities, greetings, mysteries, and feelings. From day one, babies and toddlers are showered with short bursts of words, jokes, encouragement, and questions that come endlessly and joyfully from us, the grown-ups in their world. Here in this book, you'll find action words, social words, double words, descriptive words as children really use them, all with a boost from my dear friend Mother Goose. Her unforgettable rhymes grace our language and should be a natural part of every child's early memories.

Be sure to look in the back of the book for the Word Tree, whose branches are covered with one hundred keywords and phrases. There, you will also find a list of bonus words and a list of things to search for in the pictures throughout the book.

—Rosemary Wells

Introduction

Children just love the rhymes and rhythms of nursery songs. Those verses contain many of the very first words that a child can understand and say. In this book, Rosemary Wells has chosen and adapted twenty-five classic rhymes and used them to create an utterly different approach to a child's book of first words. You'll find the keywords and phrases in colored type. These words represent all parts of speech, numbers, time, colors, actions, animal sounds, opposites, questions, and greetings. Rosemary Wells's imaginative illustrations go further to explain the meaning of each keyword, so look for a little story in pictures for each of the rhymes. Your child saying or signing their very first words is one of the shining milestones of childhood. Whether you're just starting out or well on your way, this is certain: If the language your child learns from you every day is positive, fun, and challenging, their drive to learn more will have no limit.

—Barbara Laufer, MS CCC-SLP
Codirector, Dramatic Pragmatics Speech and Language Center
Rye Brook, New York

How to get the most out of using this book with your child:

Make a lap, turn off the TV. Take it easy and have fun.

Sing, use silly voices, ask questions. Talk up a storm!

As you read, point things out in the pictures.

Make connections between what's on the page and your child's own life.

As long as your child is engaged, don't worry about speed or order.

Respond to everything with praise.

Children love repetition, so answer their demand for "More!" or "Again!"

Repetition is how they learn and remember.

GOOD MORNING!

Down at the station, early in the morning,
See the little puffer-billies all in a row.
See the engine driver pull his little lever—
Puff-puff, choo-choo, off we go!

red

blue

green

yellow

LET'S GO!

Skip, skop, to the barbershop to buy a stick of candy.
One for you and one for me and one for sister, Mandy.

for you   **for me**   **for sister**

FINDING

purple

orange

Look at this!
Look at that!
Which one has a purple hat?
Can you find an orange cat?

cat

hat

dirty

BATH

wet

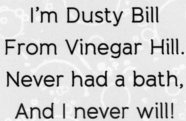

I'm Dusty Bill
From Vinegar Hill.
Never had a bath,
And I never will!

dry

clean

in

out

Mad!

MAD, MAD, MAD!

It's Sulky Sue!
What shall we do?
Give her a hug and say,
"I love you!"

Hug!

Happy!

MESS

Pudding for dessert, pudding for dessert.
Wibble, wabble, wibble, wabble,
Pudding on a plate.
Baby on the floor, baby on the floor.
Pick her up, pick her up, baby on the floor.

Uh-oh!

Oh no!

MANNERS

Hearts, like doors, have little keys,
They are *I thank you* and *if you please!*

Want!   Please!

More!

Thank you!

All gone.

COUNTING

One for the money,
Two for the show,
Three to get ready,
And four to go.

one two

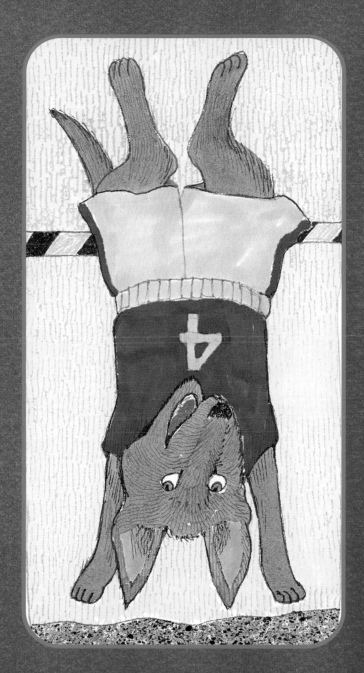

three

four

LET'S PLAY!

Maria had a little lamb,
Its fleece was white as snow,
And everywhere Maria went,
The lamb was sure to go.

dance

lie down

jump

upside down

stand

sit

climb

BIRTHDAY

Peaches, pears, apples, plums,
Tell me when your birthday comes.

surprise

Wow!

eat

all done

RAIN

Rain on the housetop, rain on the tree.
Rain on the green grass, but not on me.

splish-splash

on the roof

on the tree

on the grass

Not on me!

DOGS

Two little dogs on the top of a hill.
One named Jack and the other named Jill.
Run away, Jack! Run away, Jill!
Come back, Jack! And come back, Jill!

run away

top  **bottom**

come back

HIDING

hide

Where, oh where has my little dog gone?
Where, oh where can he be?

Where?

behind

under

Here!

KITCHEN

Pepper soup is hot.
Ice cream is cold.
Pepper soup is in the pot, nine days old.

careful

hot

cold

Yum!

ON AGAIN, OFF AGAIN

Polly put the kettle on, kettle on, kettle on.
Polly put the kettle on; we'll all have tea.
Sukey take it off again, off again, off again.
Sukey take it off again; they've all gone away.

Ready?

not ready

hat on

hat off

on again

off again

on again

off again

Goodbye!

up

down

SEESAW

Seesaw, Margery Daw.
High and low on a bale of straw.

up

down

GENTLE

I like little kitty.
Her coat is so warm.
And if I don't hurt her,
She'll do me no harm.

So I'll not pull her tail,
Not drive her away,
But kitty and I
Very gently will play.

good

sick

The cat's feeling peaky,
Weaky, squeaky.
The cat's feeling peaky.
Whatever shall we do?
We'll take him to the doctor,
The doctor, the doctor.
We'll take him to the doctor;
She'll know what to do.

help

all better

neigh-neigh

ANIMAL TALK

I have a horse,
And my horse has me.
My horse says, "Neigh!"
Under the yonder tree.

woof-woof

meow-meow

quack-quack

moo-moo

oink-oink

cluck-cluck

MY MAMA

A, B, C, my mama takes care of me. My daddy sings, "Do-re-mi!"
Eyes, nose, fingers, toes—Mama's little baby has brand-new clothes.
Close your eyes and count to ten. If you mess up, you start over again!

Mama   **Daddy**

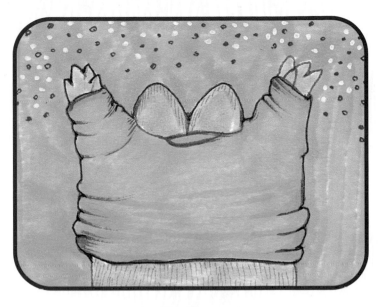

shirt

pants

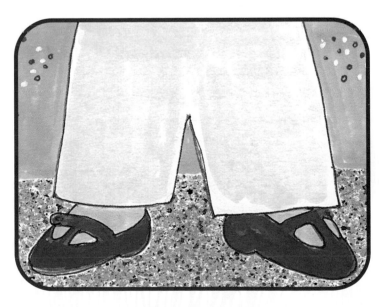

shoes

hat

CLOCK

There's a round little clock—
In the kitchen it stands.
And it points to the time
With its two little hands.
And may we, like the clock,
keep a face clean and bright,
With hands ever ready to do what is right.

wake-up time

playtime

lunchtime

clean-up time

sleepy time

fall

hurt

OUCH!

Humpty Dumpty sat on a wall,
Humpty Dumpty had a great fall.
He scraped his knee and bumped his nose,
And now he wears stickies wherever he goes.

cry

kiss

OPEN AND CLOSE

Open your mouth
And close your eyes.
I'll give you something to make you wise.

open

close

Yes!

little   **big**

MY BROTHER

My brother, Paul—he was so small.
A rat could eat him, hat and all.
He gobbled sausages and chips
And put on size around the hips.
He ate ten crumpets with his tea,
And now he's as big as ever could be.

BEDTIME

Come to the window, my baby and me,
And look at the stars that shine on the sea.

Good night!

Bonus Words

Discover these extra words as you read the rhymes.

love
book
sing
walk(ing)
honk
baby
careful
manners
time
good
look
this
pudding
sick
animal
count(ing)
bump
talk(ing)
small
grass
three
kitchen
like
hello
that
roof
orange
pull
four
coat
eat
door
mad
stars
word
see
choo-choo
kitty
gentle
birthday

Can You Find It?

Search for these everyday things in the pictures.

apple

spoon

hands

doll

moon   clock   cake

pig   chair

cow   house

cup

toys

train   lamb/sheep

feet   ball

window   ice cream

seesaw   horse

candy   table

bed   knee(s)

egg

goose   umbrella   frog

present

duck   hen

tree   shoe

Your Word Tree

For every word or phrase you have learned, count one bright green leaf on the tree. That's one hundred leaves!